The Lonely Pony

The Lonely Pony

By Sarah Hawkins

Illustrated by Jon Davis

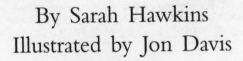

First published in the UK in 2014 by Scholastic Children's Books
An imprint of Scholastic Ltd
Euston House, 24 Eversholt Street
London, NW1 1DB, UK
Registered office: Westfield Road, Southam, Warwickshire, CV47 0RA
SCHOLASTIC and associated logos are trademarks
and/or registered trademarks of Scholastic Inc.

Text copyright © RSPCA, 2014
Illustration copyright © RSPCA, 2014

ISBN 978 1407 13968 5

RSPCA name and logo are trademarks of RSPCA
used by Scholastic Ltd under license from RSPCA Trading Ltd.
Scholastic will donate a minimum of 15p to the RSPCA from every
book sold. Such amount shall be paid to RSPCA Trading Limited
which pays all its taxable profits to the RSPCA. Registered
in England and Wales Charity No. 219099
www.rspca.org.uk

A CIP catalogue record for this book is available
from the British Library.

Printed and bound by CPI Group (UK) Ltd, Croydon, CR0 4YY
Papers used by Scholastic Children's Books are made
from wood grown in sustainable forests.

1 3 5 7 9 10 8 6 4 2

This is a work of fiction. Names, characters, places,
incidents and dialogues are products of the author's imagination
or are used fictitiously. Any resemblance to actual people,
living or dead, events or locales is entirely coincidental.

www.scholastic.co.uk

1

"Oof!" Mia woke up with a jump as something thumped on to her tummy. A familiar rumbling purr started as a large ginger cat padded down the bed, using her body like a tightrope.

"Morning!" Mia giggled as the cat walked right up to her face and gave her a hello bump with his head, his purring louder than ever. "I guess that means you want breakfast," Mia said, laughing as she stroked his soft fur and tickled him behind the ears. Marmalade nudged her again, then let out a hungry miaow.

"OK, OK, I'm getting up!" said
Mia as she threw back her covers. But
Marmalade couldn't wait. He walked to
the end of her bed and sprang up on
to her bookshelf.

"Marmalade!" Mia jumped up as he
walked along next to her books and
rosettes, knocking into everything with his
furry tail. "What are you doing!"

She jumped up to rescue him, standing

on her bed to carefully lift him off the shelf. *Miaow*, he grumbled as she picked him up, his paw sending the rosette she'd won at an under-fives' gymkhana fluttering to the carpet.

"Funny old cat!" said Mia, putting him on the bed and hanging her rosette back where it belonged. Mia smiled as she glanced round her room. It was covered in pony posters and horse-riding rosettes. *In fact*, Mia thought, looking at her room, *everyone would know she loved horses!* She had lilac-purple walls, and her curtains had purple stars on them, but everything else was covered with ponies. There were horse pictures Blu-Tacked to her bedroom walls, a pony duvet on her bed, and even her slippers were fluffy unicorns.

Miaow! Marmalade called impatiently, going to the doorway and looking back to make sure Mia was following him.

"OK, OK," Mia giggled, following Marmalade downstairs.

Down in the kitchen her mum was on the phone, walking round the table as she listened. Her long brown hair was tied up in a neat ponytail, and she was wearing her work uniform: jodhpurs, a navy polo shirt, and her blue jumper with the RSPCA logo on it.

"Mm-hm," she murmured, waving at Mia. "OK, that's great news. I'll be at the centre when she arrives. Tell the vet thanks."

Mia poured dry cat food into Marmalade's bowl and made sure he had clean water. As the tubby cat raced over to his bowl and started crunching happily, Mia poured her own cereal and tried to listen in to her mum's conversation. She must be talking to someone at the RSPCA centre where she worked.

Mia chewed impatiently as Mum finished talking. As soon as she put the phone down, Mum flicked the kettle on, and stared off into space, looking thoughtful.

"What's wrong?" Mia asked. "Is a new animal coming to the centre?"

Mum nodded. "A brown and white skewbald pony called Polly."

A new pony! Mia thought excitedly. But she knew most animals came to the RSPCA after something bad had happened to them. "Is she all right?" she asked.

"She was found on her own in a field." Mum sighed. "A member of the public called the RSPCA because they saw her

lying down. Amanda and Lindsay went
to do a rescue, and took her straight to
the vet's. She was badly treated by her
previous owner, and hasn't been fed
enough at all. In fact, the vet said she's
the thinnest horse he'd ever seen."

"Oh no!" Mia gasped.

Mum made a coffee, then came and sat
with Mia. "The vet's been looking after
her for a few weeks. She's well enough to
come to the centre now, but she's going
to need a lot of care."

Mia swooshed her cereal round in her
bowl. She loved animals so much she
couldn't bear to think about anyone
being mean to them. Marmalade gave a
miaow and jumped up on her lap. He'd
come from the RSPCA rescue centre,
too. The horse centre didn't normally
deal with dogs and cats, but he and his

brothers and sisters had been left in a cardboard box outside the front door. They had been so little that none of them had opened their eyes yet, and Marmalade had been the smallest of them all.

Mum had brought the kittens home and fed them milk every four hours until she knew that they were going to be OK. The RSPCA found all his brothers and sisters the perfect home, but Marmalade had already found his – with Mia and Mum! Mia stroked Marmalade behind the ears and he started purring happily. Looking at the big happy cat, it was hard to believe that he had ever been so tiny.

Mum came round and started doing Mia's long brown hair, combing it with her fingers and winding it into a neat plait, just like she used to plait horses' manes and tails when she was a dressage rider, before Mia was born. Mia usually loved it when Mum did her hair, but today she couldn't stop thinking about the new arrival.

"How old is she? Has she been ridden before?" Mia asked.

"She's fourteen hands high and we think she's three or four," Mum explained. "I won't know any more until I meet her later. I'm going to be her groom, so I'll be able to tell you all about her after school."

Mia didn't know how she was going to concentrate at school when there was a new horse arriving at the stables. "Polly," she said to herself. "I can't wait to meet you!"

2

"Now, since it's the last day of term . . ."
Miss Rogers paused as the class cheered.
". . . I thought we'd do a fun project.
Everyone get into pairs, and we're going
to talk about what you have planned
for your summer holidays. I want you
to practise listening to each other, and
then you'll each stand up and tell the
class what your partner is going to be
doing."

Jasmine grabbed Mia's arm. "Be my
partner?" she asked.

"Of course!" Mia grinned at her best

friend. When she and Mum had moved house last year, Mia had been nervous about starting a new school, but on the first day she'd spotted Jasmine's pony pencil case and started talking to her about horses. They'd been friends ever since! She and Jasmine were really different – Jasmine was short and Mia was tall for her age; Jasmine had short blonde hair and pink glasses, and Mia had long dark hair and freckles. Mia was quiet and Jasmine was such a chatterbox that she even talked in her sleep! But they both absolutely loved animals. Jasmine had a little white dog called Archie, who was part cocker spaniel, part poodle, so his hair was curly and he had a cute face, a bit like a teddy bear.

Jasmine pushed her glasses up her

nose and rooted around in her pencil case, bringing out a pen with a fluffy purple bit on the end. "Now," she started, holding the pencil like a microphone. "Mia Bennett, what are you doing this summer?"

Mia giggled. "Well, I'm going to be helping out lots at the centre with Mum."

"Oh, you're so lucky!" Jasmine sighed. "You've got your riding lessons," Mia pointed out. Jasmine had only just started learning to ride, but her best friend loved it just as much as she did. Jasmine went to Saddlebags, a riding school nearby, and she had already learned how to do a rising trot.

"By the end of the summer you'll probably be able to canter," Mia said encouragingly.

"I know, and I love riding Brandy," Jasmine said, "but it's only once a week. You'll be with the horses all the time."

"You can come too!" Mia promised. "The centre is going to do a summer gala this year, where people can come and learn about horses, and Mum said I can help out. We're going to teach people how to tack up properly, and show them some grooming – if they can make the horses stand still for long enough! You can come and tell people all about learning to ride."

"OK!" Jasmine said happily.

Mia wondered whether Polly had arrived at the centre yet. She could imagine Mum and the other grooms carefully getting her out of the horsebox and taking her through the yard. She hoped Polly wasn't too frightened. Horses could be very nervous in new places, but she knew Mum would be there to calm her down.

"Are you OK?" Jasmine waved a hand in front of her face.

"Sorry!" Mia stopped daydreaming. "I was just thinking about the centre. There's a new horse arriving today and she's really poorly."

"Oh no!" Jasmine's eyes went wide with worry.

 14

Mia explained about Polly being neglected and Jasmine shook her head crossly. "If anyone hurt Brandy, I'd . . . I'd set Mr Parker on them!"

Mia smiled at the thought of their strict head teacher telling off a mean owner. "I know, I hate it," she agreed. "But if anyone can make her better, Mum can."

"Right, that's enough!" Miss Rogers clapped her hands and called for attention. "Mia and Jasmine, do you want to start? Jasmine, what's Mia got planned for the summer?"

Jasmine stood up and turned to face the rest of their class confidently. "Mia and I are going to have the best summer ever," she smiled, "because we're going to spend every spare minute with horses!"

"Happy summer holidays!" Mum yelled as Mia came out of school. She was waiting in the playground next to Jasmine's mum. Archie was sitting at their feet, his tongue hanging out in a doggy grin.

Mum swept Mia up in a big hug. She'd

come straight from the stables and there were bits of hay on her trousers and in her hair.

"How's Polly?" Mia asked breathlessly. She'd been thinking about the new arrival all day long. "What's she like? Did she come out of the horse box OK?"

"One question at a time!" Mum said, smiling. "She arrived safe and sound, although she's very nervous." Mum shook her head sadly. "I think she's one of the worst cases I've seen. She's very thin indeed, but I'm going to get her on a proper diet to make her big and strong. We'll get her up to a good weight soon enough, but it's going to take something really special to make her trust people again."

Poor Polly, Mia thought sadly. "When can I meet her?" she asked.

"I need to go back and check on her

first thing tomorrow," Mum said. "You can come with me then. We'll leave her to settle in tonight."

"All right," Mia said, her mind whirling.

"Zoe and I thought we could all take Archie for a walk," Mum said, looking at Jasmine's mum.

"Yes!" Jasmine cheered.

"OK," Mia agreed, bending down to stroke Archie's curly white fur. She wished she could see Polly now, but if she couldn't meet the new pony, at least she could spend time with her favourite puppy! Archie wagged his tail as the two girls petted him, then jumped up on Mum, standing up on his back legs to sniff her trousers.

"He keeps doing that!" said Mum. "He thinks I smell like a horse."

"You do," Mia said, giving her another

squeeze and breathing in the farmyard smell on her jumper.

"Charming!" Mum replied, pretending to look cross.

"But it's the nicest smell in the world!" said Mia. She knew her mum could look really glamorous when she dressed up, but this was how she liked her best.

"Come on, let's go," Mum laughed.

"Jacob's got rugby practice with Dad, so it's just us girls," Jasmine's mum explained to Jasmine. "And Archie of course. We thought we could go for a nice walk in Holly Hill Park, then have ice creams to celebrate the start of the summer holidays."

"Oooh, yes please!" Jasmine said, turning to grin at Mia. "Can Mia come in our car?"

"But you've just been together all day!"

Mum said. "I don't know what you two find to talk about."

"Horses!" Mia said, exchanging a smile with her best friend.

They jumped in Jasmine's car, with Archie between them, Jasmine holding him safely. As they pulled up at the park Archie realized where they were and started barking excitedly, jumping around so much that his waggy tail bashed Mia in the face.

Mia giggled as she opened the car door. "Save me from this crazy dog!" she laughed.

They jumped down on to the muddy track, and Archie's white paws sank into the mud.

Mum parked next to them and opened her car door. "Now I'm glad I kept my wellies on," she said, looking down at the mud. "Here, Mia, yours are in the car boot."

Jasmine looked down at her school shoes anxiously, but her mum just laughed. "Don't worry, darling, you won't be wearing them for six whole weeks. And knowing you, they won't fit by next term anyway!"

Mia pulled on her wellies and stepped in the squelchy mud delightedly. Archie was enjoying himself, too, racing in circles around their ankles and barking happily. Jasmine's mum got a red ball out the back of their car, and clipped Archie's lead on to his collar.

Mia bent down to stroke the excited puppy, running her fingers through his curly fur. "Can I hold his lead?" she asked.

"Of course." Jasmine's mum smiled.

As soon as Mia took the lead, Archie

was off, dragging her behind him as he raced towards the gate. "Wait for me!" Mia giggled.

"Archie!" Jasmine called, running up behind them. The little dog turned around at the sound of his name, his tail wagging happily.

"Slow down," Jasmine scolded him gently. "You'll pull Mia's arm off!"

"Thanks," Mia giggled as they started walking at a normal pace. "I'm not very good with dogs – I'm much better at horses."

As they got to the duck pond in the middle of the park, Jasmine's mum bent down and took Archie off his lead for a run around.

"What do you want from the ice-cream stand, girls?" Mum said. "As if I need to ask."

Mia and Jasmine grinned at each other. They always had the same thing – the best ice cream in the whole world. "Pink and whites!" they chorused.

Mum came back with four enormous ice-cream cones, with vanilla and strawberry swirled together.

Archie came up and raced in circles around their legs as Mia and Jasmine started eating their ice creams. As the girls looked down at him, the little dog suddenly stood still, his tail wagging frantically, then raced off into the bushes.

"Archie!" Jasmine called. The bushes rustled, but there was no sign of the little dog.

"Archie!" Mia joined in. "Archie, here boy!"

The bushes rustled again, and there was the sound of frantic quacking. A duck shot out of the undergrowth, followed by a white, furry blur.

Woof! WOOF! Archie barked excitedly.

"Archie, no!" Jasmine's mum called.

But it was too late. Archie raced after the duck as it flapped away. As the duck got to the pond Mia breathed a sigh of relief. But then Archie gave a happy bark and leaped straight into the water after it!

"OH, ARCHIE!" Jasmine cried as the naughty puppy started doggy-paddling around in circles, barking happily.

3

As they arrived at the centre, Mia breathed in the smell of hay and horses and gave a huge grin. Today was the day she was going to meet Polly! Mum opened the gate, and they walked inside. Mia looked round at the familiar surroundings. There were four stable blocks around a big yard and a long wooden shed where Mum and the rest of the RSPCA grooms had their offices. Next to that was a picnic area with a little hut that they used as a shop, selling horse posters, second-hand books and ice creams to the visitors.

It was already open for the day, and Mia could see two ladies inside having a cup of tea and a chat. Two of the RSPCA grooms, Helen and Lynn, were sweeping the yard, and Ali was feeding the donkeys. Past the stables were the paddocks, and in each one, there were three or four horses, chomping the grass happily. Over in one of the training fields, Mia could see Amanda cantering Beans.

Mia grinned as she saw the little bay horse. Beans had only just arrived and still needed lots of work. He was terrified of loud noises, and couldn't go anywhere near traffic without getting really scared. But he loved his groom, Amanda, and he was getting better every day.

"I've got to call the vet, then I'm going straight up to check on Polly."

Mum nodded her head over to the isolation stables. "Give me ten minutes or so to make sure she's all right, then come and join us. Polly's in the last stable."

"OK!" Mia grinned. That gave her just enough time to say hello to all her friends! She went over to the nearest paddock and drummed her hands on the wooden fence. The three young mares, Honey, Star and Dapple, all looked up at the noise. "Hello, girls!" Mia called.

The largest mare started cantering over.

"Hi, Honey!" Mia called. The gorgeous golden palomino horse had come over to the side of the paddock to see her. Mia reached up to stroke her on the neck. Honey huffed happily, and swung her great head down so that Mia could stroke her in her favourite spot behind her ears.

Mia laughed as Honey sniffed her hands. Honey had been at the centre for six weeks, since her owner couldn't afford to keep her. She was rather greedy, and would do anything for a treat or a pat. It meant that she'd been really good and easy to train – but sometimes it made her a bit naughty, too. Once Mia and Mum had tied her up outside while they were mucking out her stable and she'd nibbled at the quick-release knot to untie herself and

gone into Star's stall to eat all her feed.
It had taken ages to drag her away!

"Hold on, I'll find you something,"
Mia said, racing back over to the stables.
She went into the feed room where the
sacks of chaff, coarse mix, nuts and hay
were kept, and found a couple of carrots.
Sticking one in her pocket, she carefully
broke the other one in half and put it in
a bucket, before going back over to the
greedy pony.

"Now, don't eat this all at once," she
said, holding out the bucket. She giggled
as the pony rushed to put her head inside
and munched it eagerly.

"Good girl," Mia said, stroking
Honey's cheek while she chewed happily,
then planting a kiss on her velvety-soft
nose.

At that moment, Dapple cantered

over to see what Honey was getting.
Mia giggled and held out the bucket to
give her a piece of carrot, too. Dapple
was a beautiful grey pony, twelve hands
high, with dark grey speckles all over
her back. She had been at the centre
for eight months. When she'd arrived
she was so wild that she'd bite and kick
at anyone that went near her, but now
she was a happy and friendly horse. Her
previous owner had ridden her in badly
fitting tack that had left sores on her
back and made her scared of saddles, so
Mum had been determined to find her
a home where she wouldn't have to
be ridden.

"Mum told me about your new home,
Dapple," she said, stroking the grey pony.
She would be so sad when Dapple left
the centre, but she was pleased that they'd

found the perfect place for her. Last night
Mum had told her that Dapple was going
to a loving home to be a companion
pony to a retired racehorse. Mia knew
that horses hated being on their own,
so it would be great for the racehorse
to have a friend, and it was a big family,
so there were lots of children to give
Dapple plenty of attention. And best of
all, nobody would ride her – Dapple was
going to love it.

Giving Dapple and Honey one more
pat, Mia went to find Mum and Polly.
Since Polly was a new arrival, she'd have
to stay up in the isolation stables for a
while to make sure that she didn't have
any germs that she could give the other
horses. There were six isolation stalls in
total, each with their own small turn-
out paddock, so the horses could still go

outside even when they weren't allowed to be with the others.

Mia's wellie boots crunched on the gravel as she raced over to the isolation stalls at the very edge of the centre. "Mum? Polly?" Mia called gently as she went towards the stall right at the end of the row. But there was no reply.

At first Mia thought the stables were empty. Usually when she went to see the horses, they put their heads over the stable doors curiously to see who was coming. *I'm sure Mum said she was in the last stall*, Mia thought to herself.

Mia almost walked right up to the stable door before she spotted her. There, cowering in the back corner, was Polly. Her ears were so far back on her head that they were almost invisible and her tail swished from side to side anxiously. She had a brown head with a white snip on her nose. Her mane was light blonde and her eyes were a gorgeous deep chocolatey brown, but they were huge and she was breathing quickly with her nostrils flared. Mia didn't need to know anything about horses to see that Polly was a scared, lonely pony.

"Hi Polly," Mia whispered. "It's OK, you're safe now," she promised.

But Polly just cowered in the corner, looking like the saddest pony in the world.

4

Mia couldn't take her eyes off Polly
as Mum slowly appeared with a
wheelbarrow. It was filled with hay and a
feed bowl with some pony nuts.

Mum came and put her arm around
Mia as she stared in at Polly. "She'll be
OK," Mum whispered. "We're going to
give her lots of love."

Mia nodded. "Why are you
whispering?" she whispered back.

"We need to be very slow and quiet so
we don't scare her." Mum explained. "To
begin with, I'm just going to sit with her

35

for a while. You stay here and be as still as possible."

Mia nodded again, hardly wanting to make a sound.

"Good girl, Polly," Mum soothed as she went inside the stable and perched on an upturned bucket. Polly shifted back uncomfortably, trying to get further into the corner. As she moved, Mia could see the brown and white patches on her body, the white stockings on all four of her legs and a white stripe down her nose. She was so thin that Mia could see her ribs through her coat. She seemed half the size of Dapple, even though they were the same age. Mia leaned quietly on the stable door, but as she looked at Polly, she felt like crying. How could anyone be so mean to such a beautiful animal?

Mum sat quietly on her bucket, looking at the floor.

"What are you doing?" Mia whispered.

"This will get her used to people being around," Mum said calmly. "It's one of the first things we work on when we're trying to teach a horse to trust people again. Do you want to hang up a hay net for her?"

Mia nodded, grateful for something

to do to help. She crept over to the wheelbarrow and started stuffing the sweet-smelling hay into an empty net.

"Where shall I put it?" Mia asked, pulling the strings of the net shut.

"You can pass it over," Mum told her. "Just move slowly so you don't scare her."

Her heart beating fast, Mia slowly passed the net into the stable. Polly shied back again, her ears twitching anxiously.

"It's OK, Polly," Mum murmured as she hung the hay net on a nail in the stable, making sure it was the same level as Polly's chest so she could get to it easily.

"I'm giving her hay rather than chaff," Mum said. "It's really important that we give her as many nutrients as possible to get her weight back to normal."

"She hasn't got many pony nuts though?" Mia said curiously, looking at the little pellets in the bucket.

Mum nodded. "She can have as much hay as she wants, but she'll have four small meals a day. Horses can't actually be sick, so we have to make sure that they don't eat too much, or they'll get stomach problems. If she eats little and often we'll soon get her back to a more normal weight."

Mia looked into Polly's beautiful brown eyes. "You're safe now, Polly," she said gently, "and you're going to have all the food you need."

She couldn't stop staring at the beautiful pony. She just wanted to stroke her and make her feel better, but she knew if she got close she'd scare Polly even more. She smiled at her gently, trying to tell her that everything was OK. Polly peered at her from under her blonde mane.

"I think she's too nervous to eat while we're here," Mum said. Slowly and carefully, she stood up. Polly backed away nervously as Mum started to move.

"OK, Polly, it's OK," Mum soothed as she came out of the stable. "That's enough stable manners for now," Mum said to Mia. "I just want to make sure she eats."

They both leaned over the door and watched. As soon as Mum left the stable, Polly warily went over to the net and started eating the hay hungrily.

"Good girl!" Mia praised her, feeling relieved.

"Well done, Polly," Mum grinned. "Come on, sweetie," she said, putting an arm around Mia. "We'd better go and get our dinner, too. Sandra and Neil have

invited us to their house tonight – would
you like that?"

"Oh, yes please," Mia said, cheering
up a bit. Sandra and Neil were her
godparents, and they'd known her since
she was born. Sandra and Mum had met
at pony camp when they were the same
age as Mia and Jasmine, and they'd been
best friends ever since. Best of all, Sandra
and Neil had two horses, Midnight and

Gypsy, as well as a black Labrador called Shadow.

Mia couldn't stop thinking about Polly as they finished their last few jobs at the centre. Before they left, she ran back over to Polly's stall, being careful not to go so close that she scared her. "Goodnight, Polly," she called softly. "See you in the morning."

As Mia left, she looked over her shoulder. Polly had her head over her stable door, watching her sadly.

Sandra and Neil's house was just a short drive away, down some winding country lanes. *Maybe one day we can ride Polly along here*, Mia thought.

Sandra waved to them from the stables as the car pulled in through the gate. She led Gypsy out into the courtyard and tied her lead rope to a loop of baling twine on a post in the middle of the yard. Then she came over to give Mum a hug.

"Hi Rachael, hi Mia." She hugged Mia next and a bit of straw from her shoulder tickled Mia's nose. "Gypsy found a nice big mud patch to roll in today, so I'm just going to groom her before dinner," Sandra explained.

"We'll help!" Mia offered. "Hi, Gypsy!" She went up to the big palomino and stroked her nose. Gypsy whickered happily. Her eyes were bright, her white-blonde tail was high and her glossy golden coat was covered with patches of dry mud. "You look like you've had a fun day!" Mia grinned, stroking Gypsy's elvety muzzle. Gypsy gave a gentle whinny, almost as if she was agreeing with Mia!

Sandra came over with the grooming kit, and they all got to work, standing on the same side of Gypsy so that she didn't get worried. Sandra started by picking her hooves out, then she began brushing her coat with a rubber curry comb, a round plastic brush with circles of plastic bristles on it. It didn't look much like Mia's hairbrush, but it was perfect for horses. Mia followed behind with a dandy brush, flicking all the dirt and mud out of Gypsy's coat. Lastly came Mum, using a soft body brush to smooth Gypsy's coat and make her nice and shiny.

"We'll soon have you looking good as new," Mia grinned.

"And then she'll go and roll in the mud again tomorrow!" Sandra laughed. "Honestly, I think she just likes being pampered." She patted Gypsy's flank and

the palomino flicked her tail happily.
"Now Midnight's getting a bit older he
doesn't want to play with her as much, so
she's finding new ways to amuse herself,"
Sandra told them.

Once they were finished, Mia helped
Sandra lead Gypsy over to her stable.

Midnight whinnied hello as they got close. "Hi Midnight," Mia called as the elderly gelding poked his head over his stable door.

"Right, we'd better go and get dinner sorted," said Sandra, once Gypsy was safely in her stall and munching contentedly on a hay net.

"Can I stay out here for a bit?" Mia asked.

"Of course," Sandra replied. "You know where the treats are!"

As Sandra and Mum went inside, Mia made sure that Gypsy's stable door was shut properly, then went to see Midnight. "Hello, boy," she said, reaching up and stroking his nose. Midnight shook his mane happily as she tickled him behind his ears.

"Now, what do we have here?" Mia said, stepping back. Pretending that she was a real RSPCA groom like Mum, she studied Midnight like she'd never seen him before. "A black gelding, sixteen hands high. . ."

She looked at the grey hairs around his ears and his droopy bottom lip. Midnight was completely relaxed, watching Mia with his tail gently swishing and his ears flicking as he listened to her voice.

"About twenty-five years old, but very healthy-looking." Mia crouched down to look at his legs and giggled as Midnight nibbled at her hair.

"I think there's only one thing that this horse needs – a sugar lump!" she finished. Mia went over to where Sandra kept them and Midnight gave a happy whicker. At the sound, Gypsy poked her head over her stable door.

"Oh you want a sugar lump, too, do

you?" Mia laughed. She fetched two out of the pot and came over to give them out.

Midnight dribbled on her hand as he eagerly gobbled down the sugar lump.

"Yuck!" Mia laughed, wiping her hand on her jodhpurs. Then the big black horse leaned forward, nosing at her other hand.

"No, naughty, this one's for Gypsy," Mia said, taking it over to where the golden palomino was patiently waiting.

As Gypsy took the treat from Mia's hand there was a shout from the house. "Mia! Dinner's ready!" Neil called.

"Coming!" Mia gave Gypsy one more pat then raced inside, her tummy rumbling.

"Mmmm!" she exclaimed as she breathed in the delicious smell coming from the kitchen. Mum was already sitting at the table, which was full of food – a big salad and huge dishes full of spaghetti and Bolognese sauce. "That was quick!"

"Chef Neil had already done it all," Sandra grinned.

"Shadow helped a bit," Neil joked, nodding at the black Lab lolling in front of the Aga.

"Hi Shadow." Mia petted him and his tail started to wag, banging against the leg of the kitchen table like a drum.

"Wash your hands," Mum said as Mia pulled out a chair. "You don't want bits of mud and horse hair in your dinner!"

"Oops," Mia said, going over to the kitchen sink. "Sorry, I was too excited. I was like Midnight with a sugar lump. It looks so yummy."

"Thank you," Neil said, pouring a Ribena for Mia and red wine for the grown-ups. "So how's my favourite goddaughter? Are you enjoying your summer holidays so far?"

"Yes!" Mia said, sitting down and digging into her spaghetti. "I spent all day at the stables. Mum's got an amazing new horse called Polly. She needs lots of help, but we're going to make sure she's OK, aren't we, Mum?"

Mum nodded.

"Well, Gypsy and I were wondering if you'd like to do some riding practice with us over the holidays," Sandra said. "If you're not tired of horses by then!"

Mia laughed. She could never be tired of horses. "Yes please!" Mia grinned as she slurped her spaghetti. This summer was going to be the best one ever!

5

It was such a bright morning that Mia couldn't help doing a little skip as she and Mum walked across the yard. She was wearing her jodhpurs, wellies and a vest top, and she could already feel the sunshine warming her shoulders. Best of all, she had the whole day to spend with Polly!

As they walked up to the offices, Mia spotted Lindsay, one of the other grooms, standing with a wheelbarrow and some fresh straw.

"Hi Lindsay!" Mum called.

"Hi guys," Lindsay said. "Mia, you're just the girl I want to see. Do you want to give me a hand mucking out?"

"Sure!" Mia grinned.

"I wish you were as keen to tidy your bedroom as you were to clean the stables," Mum laughed. Mia shrugged. Mucking out was hard work, and she knew some people wouldn't like the idea of sweeping up the dirty straw, but she loved making a nice clean bed for the horses.

"If you don't mind, that would be great," Lindsay replied. "We're very lucky to have your help – there are lots of jobs to do."

"I'm going up to see Polly," Mum called.

Oh! I want to see Polly! Mia thought to herself. Her disappointment must have shown on her face, because Mum bent down and gave her a kiss on the top of her head.

"There's plenty of time," Mum told her. "Polly's doing fine, and you've got all summer long here, don't forget – lots of time to spend getting to know her."

Mia nodded, then turned to help Lindsay. Soon she was happily forking clean, fresh straw into the stall. As she carefully spread it out, sunlight streamed through the stables and the dust from the straw shimmered in the air like golden fairy dust.

I've got all summer long! Mia hugged the thought to herself as she finished spreading out the straw in Dapple's stable, testing with the fork to make sure it was deep enough to make a nice comfy bed.

As soon as she finished, there was the sound of a horse on the gravel, and Mia looked over to see Amanda leading Beans into the yard. "Neigh!" Mia joked, poking her head over Dapple's stable door like one of the horses.

"Hi, Beans," she said cheerfully, going over to stroke the bay horse. Beans turned his head and huffed at her happily.

"He did really well today!" Amanda said, patting the frisky horse on the neck. "We had a good ride, and did lots of pole practice. When he came in, he hated anything going near his feet. But now. . ."

Leaving Mia holding Beans, she picked up a pole that was leaning nearby and put it down on the ground. Then she took the reins and clicked her tongue to call Beans forward. The horse stepped over it without even blinking.

"Well done, Beans!" said Mia encouragingly.

Just then someone started up an engine nearby and Beans whickered and started to toss his mane, kicking the pole.

"Oh Beans!" Amanda sighed as the horse danced around. "He still hates loud noises though. Let's get you rubbed

down and into your stable, mister.
Would you mind cleaning his tack for
me, Mia?"

Mia looked from Amanda to the path
up to the isolation stalls. Normally she
wouldn't mind doing anything Amanda
asked – the RSPCA groom was really
kind and had taken her out riding lots of
times – but she wanted to see Polly!

She took a deep breath and smiled at
Amanda. "Of course I'll help!" *After all,*
she thought, *Mum's right. I do have all
summer with Polly.*

Mia soon got lost in the soothing
rhythm of cleaning tack – cleaning the
reins, saddle and bridle with saddle soap
and rubbing them dry. Mum always gave
her pocket money for helping out at the
stables, but Mia liked doing the chores.
Besides, she had to learn how to do it

if she was going to have a horse of her own one day.

When she'd finished she hung everything up on the right peg in the tack room and called out to Amanda, "I'm going to go and find Mum."

"OK!" Amanda called back. "Thanks for all your help!"

Mia raced up to the isolation stables, but slowed down when she got there so that she could go quietly and carefully to Polly's stable. Mum was nowhere in sight, and all the stables were empty. Mia turned to look in the isolation paddocks. Polly was down in her field, chomping on the grass. Mia slowly walked down towards the fence, trying not to make too much noise as her wellies crunched on the gravel.

Polly looked up as she came closer,

her ears twitching anxiously.

"Hi, Polly," Mia murmured. "I've been thinking about you so much." Mia took a deep breath as she reached the fence, but Polly didn't move.

Mia stood there quietly, and Polly put her head back down to eat, her ears still pointed towards Mia nervously.

Mia waited, hardly daring to breathe, as Polly started to munch the grass, her tail swishing softly. She got closer and closer to the fence, so close that Mia could hear her chomping and chewing, and could reach out a hand and touch her.

Mia felt butterflies in her tummy. If she tried to stroke Polly, would it scare her? Would she canter off to the other side of the field? She didn't want to upset her, but she wanted to stroke her so much and show her that not all people were horrible. *I wish Mum were here to tell me what to do!* she thought.

She shifted her feet, and Polly looked up at her, her deep chocolate-brown eyes curious. Mia started talking gently, hoping that Polly would understand somehow.

"Hi, Polly," she said again. "I'm going to stroke you, OK?" As slowly as she could, she raised her hand and reached out to touch Polly on the side of her neck.

Polly stepped back and tossed her head. "It's all right," Mia soothed, "I'm not going to hurt you. Yesterday I went riding with my Auntie Sandra and her horse Gypsy. You'd like Gypsy – she's really friendly. She's beautiful, but she's not as lovely as you."

Polly looked at her and gave a quiet huff. "I want to be your friend," Mia continued, putting her hand out again. This time Polly sniffed at her hand, and then rubbed her nose against it, asking for a stroke.

"Good girl," Mia said, keeping the same calm voice, even though her heart was racing. She was stroking Polly on her nose!

There was a crunch of gravel from behind her, and Mia turned to see Mum there, watching with a big grin on her face. Mum looked from Mia to Polly and gave an amazed shrug. "Brilliant, Mia. She hasn't let me touch her much at all. She must like you!"

Mia felt a thrill of pride and tickled Polly behind her ears. She liked Polly, too!

"Last one in's a rotten egg!" Jacob yelled as he and Sam ran into the boys' changing room.

"Quick!" Jasmine shrieked. She and Mia ran into the girls' changing room and started putting their swimming costumes on as quickly as they could.

"I just can't wait to get on the flumes!" Jasmine squealed.

Mia grinned at her best friend. She'd been so excited when Jasmine had called and invited her to go to Splashdown! She'd never been to a swimming pool with slides and rides before.

"Calm down!" Jasmine's mum laughed as Mia tried to get changed quickly and got tangled up in her T-shirt. "We've got all day, there's no need to rush. Although no one wants to be a rotten egg," she added mischievously, her eyes twinkling.

Jasmine's swimming costume was yellow with flowers on it, and Mia's was blue and stripy. Jasmine had special goggles instead of her glasses, and a nose clip as well. "I dobt dike it when dhe water goes up my does," she explained. Mia giggled and grabbed her best friend's arm as they went out on to the pool side.

"Walk! Don't run. The edge of the pool might be slippy," Jasmine's mum called after them. "I'll be in the Jacuzzi if you need me." She pointed up to the round bubble pool next to the changing rooms. "Tell your brother I can spy *everything* from there, and if I see him dive-bombing he's coming straight out."

"OK!" Jasmine replied. The girls walked as fast as they could out on to the poolside, then stopped in amazement. There were huge flumes in different colours twirling down from the ceiling. Tall staircases led up to each one, and there were already queues of people waiting for a chance to whizz down and splash into the water.

A boy standing in one queue waved, and it took Mia a second to realize it was Jacob, wearing long, bright red swimming trunks.

"Hey slowcoaches!" he called. "We're

going on the deathslide! It's the black one, the worst slide in the whole place."

Mia looked at the looping black tube and shuddered. Jacob's friend Sam didn't look too happy either.

"Are you girls coming, or are you too chicken?" Jacob joked.

Mia put her hands on her hips. "Jacob Parker, if I can ride a fifteen-hand horse all by myself I'm certainly not going to be scared of a silly water slide. But Jasmine and I are going on the rubber-ring raft ride first."

Mia took Jasmine's arm and stormed off.

"You weren't really going to go on the deathslide, were you?" Jasmine asked, looking amazed.

Mia burst into giggles. "No," she laughed, "but Jacob doesn't know that!

Besides, there's no point doing something scary just to show off. And the rubber rings look MUCH more fun!"

Mia and Jasmine found their way to the huge rubber rings and picked one each. "You can get in together, girls, if you like," said the lifeguard man, holding it still so they could climb on. Mia jumped in, hanging her legs over the side. Jasmine climbed on next to her and the lifeguard gave them a push. Soon they were floating along, carried by the current, the ring twisting and turning as they gently bobbed about.

"I love summer holidays!" Jasmine sighed happily.

"Me too!" Mia grinned. "Especially now Polly's here!"

"How is she?" Jasmine asked.

"She let me stroke her," Mia told her

friend delightedly. "And Mum said I was dealing with her really well."

"By the end of the summer you might be riding her!" Jasmine grinned, trailing her hands in the water as they floated along.

"I'm not sure – it's going to take a long time for her to get better," Mia told her. But then she thought of the way Polly had nuzzled into her hand, and grinned. "But she will, I just know she will!"

After the rubber-ring ride, Mia
and Jasmine played in the main pool,
pretending they were mermaids as they
ducked and swam beneath the water.
They went in a vortex that pulled them
around in circles, and took turns jumping
over waves from the wave machine. Then
they went on the rubber-ring ride again,
racing against Jacob and Sam to see who
could reach the end of the river fastest.

By the end of the day Mia's fingers and
toes were all wrinkly from being in the
water for too long, and she was tired and
hungry, but really happy. She hoped Mum
and Polly had had as good a day as she
had!

As they drove home, Jasmine nudged
Mia. Jacob was fast asleep next to her, his
mouth open as he snored gently.

The girls giggled. "Who's the baby

now?" Jasmine whispered, and they laughed so hard that they woke Jacob up.

6

"I've got a surprise for you!" Mum
said mysteriously as they drove to the
centre.

"What is it?" Mia asked. "Is it to do
with Polly?" It had been over a month
since Polly had arrived, and Mia had seen
her almost every day.

"Wait and see," Mum laughed.

As soon as the car stopped, Mia jumped
out, her wellies sending the gravel flying
as she raced across the yard and up to the
isolation stables.

"She's not there!" Mum called.

Mia skidded to a halt. "She's not in isolation any more?"

"Nope, she passed yesterday!" Mum grinned. "She's taken Dapple's place in the paddock of young mares, with Honey and Star."

Mia glanced across the yard. There were three horses in Honey's paddock! Two of them were over by the trees, eating the grass, but one had her head over the fence of her paddock, waiting for them.

"Polly!" Mia called delightedly. Polly was almost the same size as the other horses in the field now, and she was looking happy and healthy.

Mum came over, carrying a grooming kit. "She was waiting for us!" Mia cried happily.

"She did that yesterday as well," Mum

said. "She's been getting on really well with Honey and Star, but she's such a smart pony that she likes to know what's going on at the centre, too. She's still very nervous though, so remember to be very gentle."

"Hi, Polly," Mia said, walking up to her slowly.

Mmmnnuummph, Polly whickered in reply.

Mia grinned. Polly's coat looked glossier and she seemed more alert. Her ears were forward and she watched Mia interestedly.

"Do you want to give her a little groom, Mia?" Mum asked, pointing at the brushes she'd brought with her. "I don't think she really needs it, but it'll be good for her to practise getting used to people, and she seems to really like you."

Mia felt nervous as she stepped towards Polly. "Good girl," she soothed, hoping her voice would calm Polly down as it had before. Polly didn't seem upset now, though. Her ears were pricked up, and her eyes followed Mia as she picked up a brush and slowly went into the paddock.

As Mum gave Honey and Star some attention, Mia started gently stroking the soft brush over Polly's coat, tracing the patterns of her white patches. Polly fidgeted contentedly, scratching her side against the brush. "Do you have an itch?" Mia asked, scratching the spot with her fingernails. Polly whickered happily, and turned to look at Mia.

Mia gasped as Polly pushed her face so close to hers that she could feel her warm breath on her cheek. Polly trusted her! "Look, Mum!" Mia whispered.

Mum was watching and grinning. "I knew she liked you!" she said. "Here." She passed Mia a mane comb. "See if you can detangle her mane."

Mia took the comb, but as it came closer to her face, Polly started and stomped her hooves on the ground anxiously.

"It's OK," Mia told her, slowly moving the comb closer until she could gently sweep it through Polly's mane. After a few strokes, Polly gave a deep contented huff that reminded Mia of Marmalade purring. "She likes it!" Mia said delightedly.

Polly stood still, almost falling asleep as Mia worked on the knots and tangles. A couple of times Mia tugged against a briar and Polly flinched and flicked her tail, but she didn't move away.

Mia couldn't stop smiling as she
worked on Polly's mane. It felt so special
that Polly trusted her.

Soon it was time for Polly to have
another small feed, so Mum took her up
to her stall. Mia washed her hands and
walked back into the yard, feeling like she
was walking on air.

"That was brilliant!" said Mum, giving
her a big hug. "Let me get my bag, then

I'll treat you to a celebration ice cream from the shop. Polly's going to be better in no time if you keep looking after her like that."

Mia waited in the office hallway while Mum grabbed her handbag from the office and told the other grooms about their breakthrough with Polly. Mia felt like she was going to burst with pride. As she waited, she looked up at the office pinboard, which was covered with pictures of horses in their new homes. In the middle of them all there was now a picture of Dapple with her new family. She was standing next to an old bay racehorse with kindly eyes, and was surrounded by children. She looked so happy!

One day Polly will look like that, Mia promised herself.

7

"There!" Mia gave a satisfied grin as
she jumped down from the stepladder
and looked at the sign hanging over the
centre gates.

RSPCA EQUINE CENTRE
SUMMER GALA OPEN!

It was written in big painted letters.

It had taken her and Jasmine all of
yesterday to decorate each letter with
pretty patterns, spots, stripes, horseshoes
and carrots. They'd even painted the Q

so it looked a bit like Marmalade the cat!

Jasmine jumped down off the other stepladder. "What now?" she asked.

"Well, Amanda's going to be displaying obstacle courses with Beans," Mia told her. "And Mum is doing a talk about how the animals get rehomed. . ."

"What are we doing?" Jasmine asked. "We can't be mucking out because your mum told us to wear posh clothes!" Jasmine gestured at her outfit. She was wearing her riding kit – pristine white jodhpurs, shiny boots, and a T-shirt. Mia was wearing her best riding clothes as well, and Mum had threaded a purple ribbon through her long black hair and tied it into a neat plait.

"Let's ask Mum," Mia said. They raced over to the yard, Mia's plait whipping round her face like a pony's tail. She was so excited, she had butterflies in her tummy. There were balloons and bunting hanging all around the yard, and the stables were extra neat and tidy. Lindsay was getting Star ready for her grooming demonstration, and had all the brushes lined up on a table for people to touch. Volunteers were setting up stalls and blowing up a bouncy castle in one corner of the yard, and the shop doors were open wide, the ice creams all ready for hungry visitors.

There was a sign by each horse's stall with their picture and some facts about them, telling people their name, breed, age and how they had ended up at the RSPCA. Mia felt a bit sad when she read their stories, but she hoped it would make people donate lots and lots of money!

"Ah, there you are, girls," Mum said, putting down some sparkling-clean tack as they rushed up to her.

"Now, are you two ready for your very special job?"

"Yes!" Mia said. She and Jasmine jumped up and down.

"You're going to be in charge of the donkey rides!" Mum said. "We've got it all set up so that you can take kids up and down the bridleway. But we need two very experienced stable hands to lead the donkeys."

"We'll do it!" Mia grinned.

"Oh good," Mum smiled. "We'll start a bit later, when there are a few more people, so why don't you go and have a look around first? It looks like the fete stalls are all set up, so you might find something to spend your pocket money on."

"OK!" Mia reached up on tiptoe to give her mum a kiss on the cheek, then she and Jasmine sped off.

The picnic area was full of stalls. There was a tombola and a raffle and lots of stands selling cakes and goodies that the visitors could buy. There was even a "guess the weight" of the horse competition, and the first prize was a bright-pink unicorn toy. Mia helped Jasmine guess, but she didn't spend any of her pocket money. She knew it was silly and it would take *forever*, but she was secretly saving up so that one day she could have a horse of her own. She'd never get one if she spent all her savings!

Jasmine's mum was sitting on one of the picnic benches outside the shop with lots of face paints laid out in front of her. A bright sign beside her read FACE PAINTING £2.

"Girls!" she called. "Come and get your faces painted. My treat!"

Mia and Jasmine didn't need to be told twice. They looked at each other in glee, then raced across the yard.

"What do you want?" Zoe asked. "I can do stars and swirls, or butterflies, flowers or cats. Just don't ask me to make you into horses!"

Mia and Jasmine giggled. "I don't mind," Mia said.

"OK, Mia first." Zoe patted the seat in front of her. "I'll surprise you."

Zoe held Mia's chin and carefully dipped her brush into the paint. It was cold on Mia's skin and she squirmed happily. She couldn't wait to see what she looked like!

When she was done, Mia looked at herself in the mirror. She had a bright yellow face with black stripes on it. "I'm a tiger! Thanks, Zoe, I love it!" Mia grinned. "I look just like Marmalade!"

Jasmine got a big bright-pink butterfly with its wings spread over her cheeks and antennae curling over her glasses. "Thanks, Mum, it's gorgeous!" she shrieked when she saw it.

"You're welcome," Jasmine's mum replied. "Just make sure you go round the centre and tell everyone you meet that the face-painting stand is over here. I want to raise lots of money!"

"OK!" the girls said happily.

"Are you ready, stable hands?" Mum yelled, waving from across the yard. "You look lovely!" she said as they raced over. Mum took them to the field to collect the donkeys, Milo and Patch, and lead them over to the bridleway. The centre was beginning to get busy, and there were lots of families wandering around looking at the horses. Mia even spotted a couple of people that she knew from school.

Milo and Patch trotted over when Mum called them. Mia stroked their fuzzy grey necks and big fluffy ears while Mum buckled their saddles on. When she was done, Mum gave Patch's reins to Jasmine and handed Milo's to Mia.

Jasmine laughed as she led Patch along. "I don't think I've ever walked a donkey before," she laughed. "It's a bit like walking Archie – except Patch is better behaved!"

At the bridleway, Mum had set out a

table and a sign reading DONKEY RIDES.

"So, girls," Mum explained, "the rides are for little kids only. A lot of them don't know anything about riding, so make sure that they don't kick Milo or Patch, or jiggle around too much. These guys have done lots of donkey rides, so there shouldn't be any problems, but I still need you two to be responsible handlers. OK?"

"Yep!" Mia agreed. Jasmine nodded seriously.

Mia felt really important as Mum helped a little girl put a riding helmet on, then lifted her up on to Milo's back and handed Mia the reins. The girl was about four years old, with her face painted with pink stars, and stubby plaits poking out from under her helmet. She was smiling down at Milo like she couldn't believe he was real. "Have you ever ridden before?" Mia asked as she gently led Milo along.

The girl shook her head. "I love it!" she said excitedly.

"You should ask your mum for lessons," Mia told her. "I've been riding since I was your age."

"Wow!" the little girl breathed excitedly. "Thanks, Mia!" she said as they got back to the start and Mum helped her off.

Next there was a small boy who kept pretending to be a cowboy and digging in his heels to Milo's sides. "Don't kick him," Mia explained gently. "You wouldn't like it if someone kicked you!"

"Oh." The little boy reached out and patted Milo's side. "Sorry, Milo." Milo looked at him, then threw back his head.

Uh-oh! Mia thought. *He's going to bray!*

She was used to the loud noise the donkeys sometimes made, but she knew that more than one young visitor had burst into tears when they'd heard them.

Hee-HAW! Hee-HAW! Milo called loudly.

"Shhh!" Mia patted him, but the donkey was having too much fun. Mia looked at the little boy, who was sitting on Milo's back with a shocked look on his face.

"It's OK," she said the moment Milo stopped. But the boy didn't cry. Instead, his face broke into a huge grin. "That was SO COOL!" he cried.

Mia laughed as they got back to the yard and she helped him get down. He raced over to his mum, and seconds later Mia could hear him doing an impression of Milo's noisy call.

"You look like you're having a good time!" a voice said from the queue.

Mia looked up and saw her godmother standing in line, wearing long shorts and a pink top, her hair styled in her usual neat white-blonde bob. "Sandra!" Mia grinned. "What are you doing here?"

"I wouldn't miss a pony event with my favourite goddaughter!" Sandra joked.

"I'm you're *only* goddaughter!" said Mia, smiling.

Mum came over to meet Sandra. "Let's have a break, shall we?" she asked. "Milo and Patch could do with a rest – and you girls look like you could too! Why don't you go and see Polly?"

"Oh yes!" Jasmine squealed. "We didn't get time earlier."

"I can't wait to meet the famous Polly." Sandra smiled.

"Why don't you go now," Mum told Mia. "I'll sort out the donkeys."

"Thanks, Mum! Come on," Mia said excitedly, pulling her godmother along.

Polly was standing at the other side of the paddock with Star, under the shade of the trees, but the second she heard Mia's voice she came cantering over.

"She knows you!" Jasmine exclaimed. "Brandy never does that for me."

Polly put her head over the fence

and leaned down so Mia could kiss her
on her nose. "Good girl!" Mia chatted
to her as she gave her a stroke. "Isn't she
the best horse ever?" she asked Sandra.
"I know she's still a bit skinny, but she's

getting better and better. She and Honey
and Star have become really good friends,
and she doesn't even get too scared
when strangers go near her now. She
loves it when I groom her mane, and

her favourite spot to be stroked is right *here*." She stroked the spot by Polly's ears and Polly whickered happily. "See!" Mia laughed.

Sandra had a thoughtful look on her face as she stroked Polly. "You really love her, don't you?" she asked.

"Of course!" said Mia. "I mean, I love all horses, but Polly . . . Polly is special." Polly huffed and whickered as if she was agreeing.

"Well, you certainly make a good pair," Sandra said.

Suddenly Lindsay's voice crackled noisily through the centre loudspeaker. "Could Jasmine Parker come to the guess-the-weight-of-the-horse stand and claim her prize."

"I won!" cried Jasmine in surprise.

Mia grinned at her friend. "We've got

to go, Polly, but I'll be back to put you to bed." Polly huffed and Mia gave her another kiss on the nose. "Go and play with Honey and Star," she grinned.

As Jasmine hurried them back over to the fete, Mia saw her godmother glancing back at Polly thoughtfully. But before she could ask Sandra what was wrong, Jasmine tugged on her hand.

"Come ON!" she yelled. Mia smiled and dashed after her excited best friend.

8

Mia scratched her thick grey tights. It was so weird being in her school uniform again, instead of in her old jodhpurs. The summer had gone so quickly that it felt like a dream. Now she was in Year Six, in Miss Pounds' class, and she knew it was going to be hard work. She peered out of the window and wondered what Mum was doing with Polly. Mia couldn't wait to be a grown-up so that she could work with horses all day, too!

As if she'd read her thoughts, Jasmine

leaned over and passed her a note. *How's Polly?* it read.

"She's good!" Mia whispered. "She's put loads of weight on – she's almost the same size as the other horses her age." Mia rummaged in her school bag and pulled out her mobile to find the latest picture of Polly.

"Mia Bennett." A voice boomed above her, making her jump. Miss Pounds held out her hand and Mia reluctantly put the phone in it.

"She was just telling me about Polly." Jasmine stood up for her. "She's Mia's horse. She was really sick until the RSPCA rescued her."

"That's very nice," Miss Pounds said in a voice that made it clear she didn't think it was nice at all. "But since she hasn't got anything to do with English, can you save looking at her until break time please? If you two can't behave when you sit next to each other, I'll have to split you up."

"But, Miss—" Mia started.

"That's enough," said Miss Pounds in a serious voice.

Mia stopped talking – she didn't want to be moved away from her best friend. Jasmine shot her a sorry look.

As Jasmine started writing in her exercise book, Mia realized that she had been so busy thinking about Polly, that she didn't even know what the class were doing!

"What are we supposed to do?" she mouthed at Jasmine. Jasmine rolled her eyes and pointed her pencil at the board. On it Miss Pounds had written: "A dream come true."

"Write," Jasmine mimed, pretending to scribble on her exercise book. "*One page.*" A cough from the front made Mia jump, and she put her head down and started writing.

A Dream Come True

I've only got one dream, but it will never come true. My dream is that I get to keep Polly, but I can't because looking after a horse is very expensive. Mum says that being able to look after the horses at the equine centre is almost as good as having one of our own, but it's not, because one day Polly is going to leave and go and live with someone else, and if she was mine I could keep her forever. I like all the horses at the centre, but I love Polly. She's special. She's mine.

A tear ran down Mia's nose and dropped on to the page. She rubbed her eyes with the sleeve of her jumper. Next to her she could see Jasmine making a worried face at her.

Luckily the bell went and Mia grabbed her bag and rushed outside into the playground.

"What's wrong?" Jasmine asked, giving her a big hug. "Don't worry about Miss Pounds, she's just a meanie."

"It's not that," Mia sniffed. "It's Polly. You said she was mine, but she's not really. I want her to get better, but as soon as she does she's going to find another family to live with. And I'll never see her again!"

"And then Jasmine threw her jelly at Josh!" Mia laughed as she swung on the fence.

Polly gave a whicker like she was laughing, too.

Mia reached up to stroke her velvety nose, and Polly nuzzled into her shoulder. Mia had got into a routine of coming to see Polly every day after school. Jasmine's mum dropped her off at the centre and Mum usually had a few things to finish off, so Mia got some free time to spend with Polly before she had to go home for dinner and to do her homework. She always came straight over to the paddock Polly shared with Honey and Star, and told Polly all about her day. Polly listened as if she understood every word.

"There you are! As if you'd be anywhere else," Mum said coming over, a lead rope and halter hanging from her shoulder.

"Hi Mum!" Mia called. "Is it time to go already?"

Mum laughed. "Actually, I thought we'd stay a bit late tonight and maybe grab a takeaway on the way home. Do you want to help me exercise Polly? She's healthy enough to do some lunging now. I could have done it earlier on today, but I thought you might like to watch. . ."

"Oh, yes please!" Mia jumped down from the fence.

"I thought you might say that," said Mum smiling.

Mia grinned – extra time with Polly and fish and chips too! "What do we have to do?"

"OK, I need you to hold this," Mum said, putting a carrot in a bucket and handing it to Mia. Mum took the head collar off her shoulders. Polly stepped back as she caught sight of it, and gave a wary whicker.

"Come on, Polly, remember that you get a carrot once this is on," Mum called.

"Mmm, a lovely carrot," Mia agreed, shaking the bucket.

Polly whickered again and her dark eyes sparkled. She put her head over the fence and stretched out for it impatiently.

"Here you go!" Mia held out the bucket and Polly happily put her head in, bumping her nose into the bucket to try

101

and get it. It was so different from when she first arrived and was too nervous to even eat her hay.

Mum quickly slid the head collar over Polly's nose, then buckled it behind her ears before clipping on the lead rope.

"Hurry, Mum!" Mia giggled helplessly as Polly pulled her head out of the bucket, chewing happily. "She's eaten it all!"

"OK, I'm done," Mum said, giving

Polly a pat on her neck. "There you go, that wasn't too bad, was it?"

Polly crunched down the rest of the carrot and then shook her head. Mia laughed. It was like Polly was replying to Mum's question!

"I don't think Polly is a completely green horse," Mum said, putting gloves on so that the lead rope wouldn't burn her hands if Polly pulled away suddenly.

"She's not green at all — she's brown and white," Mia joked. She knew that a "green" horse was one that hadn't had any training before.

Mia perched on the paddock fence and watched as Mum unclipped the lead rein and attached another longer line to the head collar. She'd never watched Mum work with the ponies like this, and she was paying close attention. After all, if she wanted to be an RSPCA groom like Mum, she needed to know it all. *I'm learning just like Polly!* she thought to herself.

"Walk on," Mum said to Polly, clicking her tongue. Mum started leading Polly around the paddock, gradually letting the rope out until Polly was at a lunging distance. She stood still in the middle, with Polly walking in a big circle around her.

"Let's show Mia what we learned yesterday, hey Polly?" Mum asked. As Polly walked around, Mum lifted up the lunge rein and said "whoa!" loudly.

Polly hesitated, her ears flicking interestedly, then stopped.

"Good girl!" Mum praised her.

"Well done, Polly!" Mia called.

"Now, walk on!" Mum commanded.

Polly took a step forward, then glanced at Mia warily, her tail swishing from side to side.

"Go on, Polly!" Mia cheered.

Mum walked her round a few more times, first in one direction and then in the other. Polly walked, stopped, and turned perfectly.

"Good job, Polly," Mum said finally. She

unclipped the lunge rein and reattached the lead rope, then tied Polly up to a loop on the fence.

"At this rate, she'll be ready for a new home in no time," Mum said cheerfully. Mia rested her face against Polly's neck and sighed. She wanted Polly to get better, but she couldn't bear the thought of her leaving. . .

9

Mia held her breath as Mum put her foot in the stirrup.

"Easy, girl," Mum soothed. With one smooth movement, Mum swung her leg over Polly's side and sat down on the saddle.

Polly shifted back a bit, her ears low, but she didn't seem too upset by the funny weight on her back. She trusted Mia and Mum so much now, and she knew they'd never do anything to hurt her. Mia stroked her nose and offered her a bit of carrot from the bucket, trying to seem calm even though her heart was racing. *Polly was doing so well!*

Mia knew that over the last few weeks Mum had got Polly used to the saddle, and had even been out on a few short rides, but it was amazing to see it for herself. The horse in front of her looked so different from the one that had come to the RSPCA equine centre all those months ago. Her coat was thick and she was sleek and healthy – she even had a little tummy!

Now that Polly's weight was back to normal, Mum had been doing more and more work with Polly. This weekend she had suggested a special treat: that she and Mia take Polly and one of the other ponies on a hack along the bridle path next to the centre.

Just then, Star, the pony Mia was going

to ride, whinnied as if to say, "Don't forget about me!"

"Don't worry, Star, there's a carrot for you, too." Mia turned to where the little spotty Appaloosa horse was hitched up to the gate, and gave her a piece of carrot. Star had been at the centre for almost a year now, and was ready to be adopted. Mum and the other grooms were already looking for her perfect family. Star was so patient and kind-hearted that Mia was sure she'd find a home soon.

"Right," Mum said. "Let's get going!"

Mia untied Star, checked her stirrups and girth, then carefully climbed up on to her back. "Good girl," she said, patting her on her neck. Mia had ridden Star lots of times before, but she still felt a tiny bit nervous as she looked over at Mum and Polly.

She wished that she could be riding Polly herself, but she knew that Polly was still learning. Horses had to learn how to be ridden just like people had to learn how to ride. When they were first taken out they could spook at loud noises and traffic whizzing past them, as well as other animals in nearby fields – even a flapping sheet on a washing line or a plane flying overhead could scare them. Today, though, it should be safe because they were only going down the bridleway.

"Ready?" Mum asked.

Mia nodded. Mum clicked her tongue and squeezed her legs to make Polly go. Polly moved over to the gate, but when Mum tried to get her to turn on to the path, the skewbald horse wouldn't go.

"Come on, Polly," Mum said, holding the reins softly, but Polly still pulled against her, turning her head back to look at Mia, sitting on Star.

"Mia's coming, too!" Mum laughed. "Look, she doesn't want to go without you. You go first, Mia."

Even though Polly was being naughty, Mia couldn't help feeling pleased. All the grooms had commented on the fact that Polly loved Mia best, and it made her feel so special.

She clicked her tongue to make Star walk out of the gate, and this time Polly followed happily, walking smoothly.

Mum and Mia rode their horses side by side down the bridleway, the horses' breath coming out in clouds and wintery sunshine filtering through the golden and red autumn leaves. Riding down the country track, feeling Star gently rocking her as she strode along and seeing Polly next to her, Mia felt happier than she could ever remember.

They moved into a slow trot, and for a while there was just the sound of the horses' hooves and the birds singing in the trees.

"Shall we stop for a bit?" Mum said as

they came to a stream. Mum slid off Polly's back and helped Mia down. Mia gave Star a thank-you pat, then loosened her reins so she could bend down to the water to drink.

"Do you want to sit on Polly?" Mum asked.

Mia caught her breath as butterflies danced in her tummy. She wanted to ride Polly more than anything, but she felt nervous too. *What if Polly didn't like it? It had taken her so long to trust people, what if Mia messed it up?*

Mum smiled as if she could read Mia's thoughts. "Don't worry. She's been doing so well, and the two of you have a real connection. It'll be fine."

"OK," Mia gulped.

Polly looked completely relaxed, her tail swishing gently from side to side. She huffed happily as she bent down to nibble some long green grass from the side of the stream.

Mum took Star's reins and gave Polly's to Mia. Mia slowly walked closer, murmuring to Polly as she stroked her neck. Then, taking the reins, she put one hand on the saddle and placed her left foot in the stirrup before carefully swinging herself up.

Polly gave a surprised huff, and swung her head round to look at Mia, as if she was thinking *what are you doing there?*

Mia leaned forward and smoothed Polly's mane calmly, but inside she wanted to scream and shout. *I'm sitting on Polly!* she thought delightedly.

Mum nodded approvingly. "Good work, Mia!" she said. "Now, why don't you try a little walk—" Mum was interrupted by the rev of an engine as a car went past nearby. Both horses jerked their heads up, their ears pricked forwards.

Star went back to drinking the water, but Polly's eyes rolled and she gave an anxious squeal as she started to panic. Desperately, Mia reached forward and tried to soothe her with her voice and her hands. "It's OK," she murmured. "It's just a noise. It's far away, it can't hurt you. I promise you're safe, Polly."

"Well done, keep talking," Mum said softly.

Mia stroked Polly's neck as the pony slowly settled down. Her breathing got steadier, and she stopped pawing the ground. She was still looking round worriedly, but she didn't look like she was going to bolt away.

Mum came over and helped Mia down. Mia's knees were all wobbly as she stood next to Polly. Even though she'd done lots of riding, nothing like that had happened before. She'd thought Polly was going to run away with her clinging on to her back! Worst of all, she hated the thought of Polly being scared.

"You were brilliant, Mia," Mum said, giving her a quick hug. "Even experienced horses would have spooked –

but you helped her stay calm."

"We helped each other!" Mia said with a smile, as Polly whickered in agreement.

10

"I've made your favourite for dinner tonight," Mum said as she and Mia walked in the front door. "I thought we could eat it on our laps in front of the TV for a treat. We can snuggle up on the sofa and watch a film."

"Great!" Mia said, dropping her school bag and racing up the stairs to get changed. Marmalade was curled up in the middle of her bed like a big furry hot–water bottle. When he saw her he gave a happy miaow and flipped over on to his back so that Mia could rub his tummy.

"Hi, Marmalade." Mia perched on her bed to rub his furry belly. He squirmed and started a deep rumbling purr.

"Come on, Mia!" Mum called from downstairs. Mia jumped out of her clothes and got straight into her pyjamas. They had a pattern of blue, purple and red ponies galloping all over them and they were fleecy and warm. "Mum said I should be cosy," she giggled as Marmalade gave her a curious look. "Come and cuddle up with us," she said, picking Marmalade up and cradling him like a baby. He snuggled into her arms happily as she took him downstairs. Mum had got everything ready, but instead of sitting cosily on the sofa, she was standing in front of the fireplace.

"Ha! I've got the best spot!" Mia crowed, sitting down and pulling the blanket over her legs. Marmalade padded around, then settled in a ball on her lap.

Mia expected Mum to laugh and barge over next to her and start a tickling fight. But instead Mum turned to her with a really serious expression on her face.

"What's wrong?" Mia asked. "Mum?"

Mum sat down on the edge of the sofa and started stroking Marmalade's fur. Then she took a deep breath and looked at Mia. "Sweetheart, you know Polly's been doing really well?"

"Is she OK?" Mia asked, a bolt of cold fear shooting through her.

"Yes, yes she's fine," Mum reassured her. "In fact, she's so good that we're going to start looking for a home for her."

Mia gasped. It had been so long since she'd thought about Polly leaving. She'd just tried to pretend it wouldn't happen.

She stared down at Marmalade, running her fingers through his fur. Her tummy felt like it was tied up in knots inside.

"Oh, sweetie." Mum put her arm around her and pulled her in close. "You know how expensive it is to keep a horse," she said gently. "We just can't afford it. But the RSPCA are going to find the *perfect* home for her – I'm going

to make sure of it. We've already got a list of people and we'll meet them all and make sure that Polly gets matched with someone that will really love her. Isn't it nice that she's healthy enough to go to a family of her own?"

Mia nodded, but she couldn't help a salty tear rolling down her face and dripping off her nose. *Polly already had someone who really loved her.*

As tears started to patter down on to his fur like raindrops, Marmalade turned around and gave her a confused look. He sat up, stretched, and rubbed his head against Mia's chin, like he was drying her tears. "Oh Marmalade," Mia sobbed, burying her face in his fur. "What am I going to do?"

She couldn't bear the thought of Polly being taken far away — she'd never see her again!

"It'll be OK," Mum promised. "Come on, let's try and have a nice girly evening. You can choose the film."

But all Mia could think about was Polly. She leaped up so fast that Marmalade jumped off her lap with a surprised miaow.

"Mia—" Mum called out, but Mia didn't stop. She raced upstairs to her bedroom and flung herself on her bed.

All around her bedroom, where there used to be pictures of horses she'd cut out of magazines, now there were photos of Polly. Mia pulled the closest one off the wall and stroked her fingers over Polly's light mane. This one was from a couple of months ago, on Mia's birthday. She'd asked for a carrot cake especially so that she could make a similar one for Polly out of carrots and chaff. In the photo, Mia was holding up her cake and Polly was next to her, nibbling hers out of her feed bucket.

Mia knew that it was a good thing that Polly was so much better. She just wished that she could keep her.

Sniffing, Mia dried her eyes on her pyjama sleeve. Suddenly she had an idea. Even if she couldn't keep Polly, she *could* show her how much she loved her. . . She jumped up and grabbed her piggy bank off her desk, then started shaking it out on to the floor. She'd saved every bit of her pocket money she'd ever got. She knew it wasn't anywhere near enough for her own horse, but there was enough to do something special – buy Polly a present.

She ran downstairs to find one of Mum's horse magazines. She'd seen the perfect thing. Mia flicked through the pages until she found what she was looking for. It was a set of purple heart-shaped brushes for grooming, all in a lovely glittery purple kit box. Polly's new owner might not know how much she enjoyed having her mane brushed. And there was a matching head collar and lead rein, too. It was the same purple colour as Mia's bedroom.

"Mum, can I get these for Polly?" she asked breathlessly, rushing into the kitchen.

Mum looked at the page. "All of this? But that's nearly seventy pounds!" she said. "Have you saved all this from your pocket money?"

Mia nodded. "My pocket money and the birthday and Christmas money Grandma sends me. I was saving up so I can get a horse one day, but I want to get something for Polly now," she said. "And . . . and she needs to look nice so that the best people will adopt her."

"Oh Mia!" Mum opened up her arms to give her a hug. Mia fell into her mum's arms and sobbed.

11

"Thanks, Zoe!" Mia called as they reached the centre. "You can drop me here."

"Are you sure?" Jasmine's mum looked at the rain lashing down. The windscreen wipers were going back and forth with a squeaky whooshing sound, but they still weren't going fast enough to keep the window clear.

"It's OK. I'm just meeting Mum at the gate," Mia told her. "I've got an umbrella."

Jasmine's mum looked at her watch.

 127

"OK," she said hesitantly. "I hate to leave you in this weather, but I've got to take Josh to rugby practice, and if I don't leave now we'll be late."

"It's fine, honestly," Mia said cheerfully. "Thanks for the lift."

"You're welcome, love. Say hi to your mum for me," Zoe replied.

"And say hi to Polly from me." Jasmine reached over and gave her a sympathetic hug. She knew all about Polly getting rehomed, and she knew how upset Mia was. She'd tried to cheer her up by talking about all the new horses that would be coming to the rescue centre, and the lovely life Polly was going to have. Mia was determined to try and think about all the good things – that Polly was happy and healthy now, and she'd have a home where she'd be loved. That was the most important thing.

Mia opened the car door and jumped out. The rain was pattering down in fat drops, but she was nice and dry under her umbrella. She got out her phone and looked again at the text message Mum had sent her at break time.

Meet me at the front gates. Don't go into the centre. I want to leave as soon as I finish work. Love you lots, Mum x

There was still ten minutes before Mum finished her shift. *Just enough time to see Polly and give her a quick nose rub*, Mia thought.

Mia slung her school bag over her shoulder and opened the gate, squelching through the mud towards the yard. There was a light on in the little shop, but there was no one in the rainy yard. Mia rushed through, avoiding the puddles and trying not to get her school shoes too muddy.

As she went past each stable a friendly horse looked out to greet her, looking surprised that she was walking around in the rain. Most of them were already back in their stalls for the night, and the ones who lived in the fields were sheltering under the trees at the other end of their field. They were native ponies with thick coats, and Mia knew that the rain didn't bother them.

Mia walked over to Polly's stall. The rest of her friends were in their stalls, too, munching happily on hay. Honey whickered as she came nearer. "Shh, I'm not meant to be here," Mia laughed,

reaching up to give her a quick pat.
"I've snuck in to visit Polly — don't tell
Mum!" Honey huffed quietly as if she
understood, then went back to eating
her dinner.

Mia squelched on to Polly's stall. "Hi,
Polly!" she whispered, then stopped,
a horrible feeling spreading from her
head to her toes. "Polly?" she whispered.
But Polly's stall was completely empty,
cleaned out ready for the next horse.
Polly had gone.

★

Mia walked back to the gate in a daze. She couldn't believe Polly had already gone. Usually it took a while for the RSPCA to find each horse just the right home. The new owners had to have lots of checks and be visited by an RSPCA officer before they were allowed to come to the centre and meet the horses. Even after they'd taken the perfect pony home, an RSPCA inspector went to do a home visit before it was officially theirs. Mum had only been looking for an owner for Polly for a few weeks . . . and she was already gone.

Mia had been back at the gate for a few minutes when Mum appeared. "Ah, there you are!" she said brightly. "Are you ready to go? We're going for dinner at Sandra and Neil's house."

Mia nodded numbly. Mum was probably going to tell her about Polly over dinner. That was why she'd wanted her to wait at the gate. She and Sandra and Neil were probably going to be really kind and nice, but there was nothing they could say that could make things better. Polly was gone, and she hadn't even been able to say goodbye.

Mum sang along with the radio as they drove the short distance to Sandra and Neil's house. Mia just stared out of the window at the rain pelting down. The inside of the car got all steamy. "What mis-er-able weather!" Mum said cheerfully. "Still, it'll be lovely and cosy at Sandra's."

Mia shrugged miserably. She started tracing Polly's name in the mist on the window, then stopped as tears prickled her eyes.

"Here we are," Mum said as they pulled into the driveway. "Oh and look, Sandra and Neil have come out to meet us." Sandra and Neil were standing at the front of the house, under huge umbrellas. Neil was grinning widely as he came over to meet them at the car door.

"Your umbrella, m'ladies," he joked, holding it over them as they got out.

The adults grinned at each other, but Mia was silent as she trudged through the rain towards the house.

"Aren't you going to say hello to Gypsy and Midnight, Mia?" Sandra asked. "You normally go straight over there."

Mia turned to the stable block, then stared in amazement. She could barely believe her eyes. There weren't two horses peering out, but three. Next to Gypsy and Midnight, there was a familiar white and brown pony. Polly!

"What?" Mia looked from the horse to Sandra. It *was* Polly, with her light mane, twinkly chocolate-brown eyes and the white blaze on her velvety nose. But what was she doing here?

"Well, Midnight's getting old, and

Gypsy needed a companion. . ." Sandra
started to explain. "We were thinking
about getting a new horse, and when I
saw you with Polly. . ."

"But why is she here?" Mia stuttered.

"We're the ones who have adopted
her!" Sandra grinned. Mia couldn't
speak as she looked from the horse to
her godmother in confusion. It was too
amazing to be true.

"It was so obvious that you and Polly
have a special connection, darling. When
I saw her with you, well, she's pure love,"
Sandra said.

The rest of what she was going to say
was smothered as Mia flung herself into
her godmother's arms.

"Thank you, thank you, thank you!"
she sobbed. "I went to see her today and
I saw her empty stall. I thought she'd

been rehomed and I hadn't got to say goodbye."

"Oh Mia!" Mum protested. "That's why I didn't want you to go inside. You didn't have to worry."

"You *never* have to say goodbye now," Sandra said, kissing the top of her head. "She's here to stay, and you can see her whenever you want."

"I kept wishing and wishing that I could keep her somehow," Mia sniffled. "I can't believe my wish came true!" Mum came and put her arms around Sandra as well.

"What about me?" Neil jokingly complained.

"Join in!" Mum grinned, opening up her arms. They had a big group hug, and then there was a whinny from the stables.

"Polly!" Mia gasped. "Does she know

she's staying?"

"She was a bit confused when we put her in the stable," Mum said. "You'd better go and tell her."

Mia wriggled out of the hug and raced over to the horses. The rain poured down on her but Mia didn't care. She'd never felt so happy in her whole, entire life!

Polly gave a soft whinny as Mia ran over to her.

"You're staying here!" Mia told her. "You're staying with me!"

Polly put her head down and Mia looked into her big gorgeous eyes. She knew Polly understood every word she said.

"You're going to live here and I can see you every day! Well, when Neil and Sandra say it's OK."

The adults walked up behind her. Mum and Sandra had their arms around each

138

other, and they were all grinning.

"You can come round as much as you like," Neil smiled. "We got her for you. And we can always use a stable hand."

Polly nudged Mia with her nose, and Mia turned to wrap her arms around the beautiful pony's neck. Polly gave a great huff of contentment. From the next stable, Gypsy poked her head out and gave an answering whinny.

"We introduced them when Polly arrived," Sandra told Mia, "and they got on brilliantly. It looks like they're going to be great friends."

Polly turned back to Mia and put her head down, nuzzling into her shoulder lovingly. She huffed gently, like a happy, contented pony.

"She knows," Mia said, looking at Polly's deep chocolate-brown eyes. "She knows she's come home."

12

"And the next contestant is . . . Mia and her skewbald pony, Polly!" The voice over the tannoy boomed across the sunny field. Mia felt her heart jump with joy. She leaned over and stroked Polly's neck and Polly gave an excited neigh. They'd been practising this for so long, and Mia knew Polly was excited and ready to go. Her mane and tail were plaited and tied with the same purple ribbons that Mia had threaded through her own hair.

Mia glanced over to where the audience were watching. Everyone was there – Mum, Sandra, Neil and Shadow. Jasmine was jumping up and down excitedly and her mum waved as she held Archie on his lead. Lindsay and Amanda were there, too, in their RSPCA uniforms. They were giving a talk about the charity, but they'd all stopped to come and cheer Mia and Polly on. Polly was one of their success stories – a happy, healthy pony who, thanks to the work of the RSPCA, had a loving home and a brilliant new life.

"Go!" the tannoy announced. With a click of her tongue and a press of her knees, Mia urged Polly forward. Polly trotted out into the performance area, moving smoothly beneath her. Mia was completely focused on her horse, holding her breath as Polly did everything she asked her to.

They'd done the routine so many times that Mia could do it in her sleep. First they had to slalom in and out of some barrels, then cross the field diagonally before coming back and walking over some poles. Then it was another turn, back around the barrels, and they were done.

"Good girl," Mia muttered as Polly trotted past the first barrel confidently. She touched Polly's flank with her right heel and Polly smoothly turned to the right round the next one.

Mia gently pulled the reins to turn left, but Polly was overexcited and she kept going, shooting past the next barrel.

"Doesn't matter, keep going," Mia soothed, but Polly didn't seem worried at all. In fact, she was having a brilliant time!

"An almost perfect display there from

Mia and her skewbald pony, Polly!" the announcer said as they finished. Mia trotted Polly out of the arena, grinning with pride. They'd done it, their very first gymkhana event together, and Polly had been brilliant!

"Well done, Polly," Mia said happily, stroking her neck. Polly whickered contentedly – and turned back towards the field as if she wanted to go round again!

"Come on, Polly, let's go see everyone," Mia urged. Their friends and family crowded round as Mia jumped out of the saddle and slid to the floor, straight into her mum's arms.

"You were fantastic!" Mum grinned, kissing the top of her head. "And you too, Polly, of course," she added, catching the reins and planting a kiss on Polly's nose.

"That was brilliant!" Jasmine squealed. "You're going to be placed for sure."

Mia grinned as she took off her riding helmet. "I don't know. I'm just glad we did it, and Polly enjoyed it."

"She certainly did," said Sandra, stroking Polly's velvety muzzle. "And you handled her brilliantly."

"Contenders in the under-twelve category, please assemble for the results!" the voice said over the tannoy.

Mum squeezed Mia's hand, then Mia led Polly back into the field and lined up with the other girls and their horses.

Jasmine held up her crossed fingers as the judges came out clutching a handful of colourful rosettes.

Mia felt her tummy wobble nervously. But then Polly put her head down and nudged her shoulder and Mia felt all her worries disappear. As long as she had Polly, nothing else mattered.

Mia clapped politely as the second and third place ribbons were given out. Finally, it was time to announce the winner.

"First prize. . ." the judge started.

Mia held her breath. She couldn't have won – she and Polly had made a mistake. . .

". . .to Helen and her bay mare, Mull!"

"Yes!" the girl next to Mia shrieked as she was awarded a huge red ribbon.

"Never mind," Mia said, stroking Polly's neck. "It was our first try. We'll place next time."

The judge put his hand up and the noise from the crowd calmed down. "There is one more prize for this category," he said with a smile. "For the best relationship between an animal and their rider. This pair have been through a lot. Not long ago, this pony came to the RSPCA in a terrible state."

Mia gasped. They were talking about Polly!

"Through their hard work," the judge

147

continued, "and the love of a particular young lady, Polly is now a beautiful, capable pony, and looks set to be a very good contender one day. The bond between them is so strong, that we felt we had to commend it. This was a very lonely pony, but she's certainly not any more. We'd like to award this highly commended ribbon . . . to Mia and her skewbald pony, Polly."

Everyone around them burst into the biggest round of applause yet. Mia felt like crying as she hugged Polly. The judge handed her a beautiful purple rosette. "Well done," he said, his eyes twinkling. "Next time, you'll have a winner's rosette, mark my words."

"Thank you," Mia stuttered as she looked down at the rosette on her jumper. The judge gave her a matching one, which she proudly pinned on Polly's bridle.

Over in the audience, Mia could hear her family shrieking and see Jasmine and Sandra jumping up and down. But there was only one person she cared about right now. She put her arms round Polly's neck and gave her a hug. "We'll put that on your stable door when we get home," Mia promised. "And we can show Gypsy and Midnight – they'll be so happy. Next year we'll compete again. . ." Mia grinned, "and every year if we want, because we'll always be together."

Polly whinnied in agreement

Their family and friends ran over and surrounded them happily, all talking at once. *The judge was right*, Mia thought as she hugged her horse. *Polly would never be lonely again. And neither would she.*

The Real-Life Rescue

Although the characters and animals in Mia's story are fictional, they are based on a real-life rescue.

Polly, a three-year-old skewbald horse, was shockingly thin when she arrived at Felledge Equine and Animal Centre.

Because she hadn't eaten properly for so long, Polly was half the weight she should have been when she arrived at the centre.

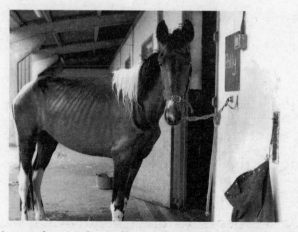

Photo by Andrew Forsyth/RSPCA Photolibrary

An underweight Polly at the start of her recovery

She was given a special diet, and the amount of food she received was increased gradually so she didn't get colic (a potentially fatal stomach condition).

As well as helping Polly gain weight and improve her health, work began to help her trust humans and teach her "stable manners", including allowing people to enter her stable, simple voice commands and having her feet picked up.

Rachael Duffy, a groom at the centre, was in charge of her training, and spent many hours with Polly, trying to gain her trust. She said:

"Polly would put her ears back when you went near her and didn't like anyone being in the stable when she was eating. But after a few weeks of working with Polly, she began to understand that I was there to help. Suddenly she started waiting for me at the field gate when it was time to come in."

After six months, Polly was ready to for staff to see if she could be trained to be ridden. This was done in a gentle and gradual way, by introducing new experiences and building up Polly's confidence.

Nine months after Polly arrived at the centre, Rachael sat in the saddle for the first time.

Photo by Joe Murphy/RSPCA Photolibrary

Groom Rachael Duffy riding Polly for the first time

Rachael says:

"Polly is perfect now. She loves cuddles and kisses and is a lovely horse to be around."

Polly loves kisses!

To find out more about the work
the RSPCA do, go to:

www.rspca.org.uk

9/14